P9-DYE-667

08/16

Ms. Krup Cracks Me Up!

Dan Gutman

Pictures by
Jim Paillot

HarperTrophy®
An Imprint of HarperCollinsPublishers

To Emma

Ms. Krup Cracks Me Up!

Text copyright © 2008 by Dan Gutman

Illustrations copyright © 2008 by Jim Paillot

All rights reserved. Printed in the United States of America.
No part of this book may be used or reproduced in any manner whatsoever without
written permission except in the case of brief quotations embodied in critical articles
and reviews. For information address HarperCollins Children's Books, a division of
HarperCollins Publishers, 195 Broadway, New York, NY 10007.

www.harpercollinschildrens.com

Library of Congress Cataloging-in-Publication Data is available.
ISBN 978-0-06-134605-7 (pbk.) — ISBN 978-0-06-134606-4 (lib. bdg.)

Typography by Joel Tippie

❖

First Harper Trophy edition, 2008

16 17 18 19 20 OPM 24 23 22 21

Contents

1 Field Trips Are Boring 1

2 Weird People 5

3 The *Giganotosaurus* 10

4 Wild Yak Attack 19

5 The Scary, Dead Zombie Buffalo 28

6 The Hall of Dinosaurs 37

7 It's Alive! 43

8 We Have a Problem 51

9 Slinking Around 59

10 Penguins Are Cool 69

11 How to Stuff Stuff 74

12 The Amazing World of Poop 81

13 Stuff Like This Happens Every Day 92

Field Trips Are Boring

My name is A.J. and I hate school.

It was Monday—the worst day of the week. We were on our way to lunch in the vomitorium at Ella Mentry School. My friend Ryan Dole was the line leader. I was the door holder. All the guys were talking about the big football game that was on TV over the weekend. All the girls were gabbing about some girly stuff, like what color shoes they have.

"Enough chitchat!" said our teacher, Mrs. Daisy.

Mrs. Daisy used to be *Miss* Daisy, but she went off and got married to our reading specialist, Mr. Macky. So now we call her Mrs. Daisy.

"I just got some great news!" she told us. "Next week our class is going on a field trip!"

"Yay!" yelled all the girls.

"Boo!" yelled all the boys.

Ugh! I remember the last time we went on a field trip. It was totally lame. Do you know why? We went on a field trip . . . to a *field*! How lame is that? We had to look at disgusting bugs. Our science teacher, Mr. Docker, even *ate* one of them. But then, Mr. Docker is off his rocker.

We should go on a field trip to an amusement park or a video arcade. That would be cool.

"I love field trips!" said this annoying girl with curly brown hair named Andrea, who loves everything teachers love.

"Me too!" said her crybaby friend, Emily. "Where are we going?"

"We're going to visit a natural history museum!" Mrs. Daisy said, all excited.

WHAT?! A natural history museum?

Natural stuff is boring.

History is boring.

And nothing's more boring than a museum.

So a natural history museum is sure to be the most boring place in the history of the world!

Now you know why I hate school.

Weird
People

I grabbed a lunch table in the vomito-rium with the guys. Andrea and some of the girls sat at the next table.

Michael, who never ties his shoes, put straws in his nostrils and said he was a walrus. Neil, who we call the nude kid

even though he wears clothes, put Tater
Tots over his eyeballs. Ryan balanced his
lunch box on his head.

"Ugh, broccoli!" I said as I opened my lunch bag. "I'm not eating food that looks like a tree."

"I'll eat it," said Ryan, who will eat anything. Ryan even eats stuff that isn't food. He's weird.

"I don't want to go to a natural history museum," Michael said.

"What a snore!" I told the guys. "I bet they're going to tell us the history of rocks."

"Hey, rocks are cool," said Neil the nude kid. "I have a rock collection at home."

"You collect *rocks*?" I asked Neil. "Why collect something that's just lying around on the ground? You might as well collect air."

"My uncle collects air," Ryan said. "Whenever he goes on a trip, he brings an empty bottle along. He's got bottles of air from all over the world."

"Your uncle is weird," I told Ryan.

"One time he couldn't find a bathroom and had to use one of his bottles," Ryan added.

"Ew, gross. See? I told you he was weird," I said.

That's when Little Miss I-Know-Everything opened her big mouth at the next table.

"Natural history isn't just about rocks and air, dumbheads!" she said. "It's about *all* the objects in nature, like plants and animals."

"So is your face," I told Andrea.

Any time any-body says some-thing mean to you, just say "So is your face." That's the first rule of being a kid.

I wish some plants and animals would fall on Andrea's head. Like a 400-pound piece of broccoli, and a hippopotamus.

The Giganotosaurus

"Bingle boo!" said our bus driver, Mrs. Kormel. "Limpus kidoodle!"

"Bingle boo!" we all said, as we piled onto the bus.

Mrs. Kormel invented her own secret language. So instead of just saying "Hello" and "Sit down," she says "Bingle boo" and "Limpus kidoodle."

Mrs. Kormel is not normal.

I had to lug my sleeping bag with me, because we were going to be spending the whole night in the natural history museum. Just what I always wanted to do, sleep next to boring dead stuff.* At least I had my Batman sleeping bag. Batman is cool.

There were some grown-ups on the bus with us too. Mrs. Daisy and Mr. Macky and Mr. Docker were all there. Ryan's mom, Mrs. Dole, came along as a chaperone. That's a fancy word that means "a

---

*Our parents had to sign permission forms before we could go. That way, if something dead came back to life and attacked one of us, it would just be too bad.

grown-up who hangs around with kids to make sure we don't have any fun."

"Are we there yet?" I asked Mrs. Kormel as soon as she started driving.

"No, A.J.," she said.

I kept asking Mrs. Kormel every five minutes if we were there yet. Any time you're in a car or bus, always ask if you're there yet—even if you know perfectly well that you're *not* there yet. That's the first rule of being a kid.

It took a million hundred hours to get to the natural history museum.

"Pinkle burflenobin!" announced Mrs. Kormel when the bus finally stopped.

That means "Everybody get off the bus"

in Mrs. Kormel's secret language.

As soon as we walked into the museum, we heard an announcement: "The museum will be closing in five minutes."

"Yay!" I shouted. "We can go home!"

"That means everybody *else* has to go home, Arlo," said Andrea.

"I knew that," I lied. I hate it when Andrea calls me by my real name.

In the entrance of the museum, I looked up and saw the most amazing thing in the history of the world! It was a huge dinosaur skeleton that just about filled the whole room! Dinosaurs are cool.*

---

*Not as cool as penguins, but still cool.

"WOW!" everybody said, which is "MOM" upside-down.

"It's a *Giganotosaurus*!" said Andrea. "He was one of the biggest meat-eating dinosaurs in the world—even bigger than *T. rex*!"

"That's right, Andrea!" said Mr. Docker. "How did you know that?"

"I read about the *Giganotosaurus* in my encyclopedia," said Andrea, all proud of herself. "He weighed eight tons!"

"He should have gone to Weight Watchers," I said. "My mom

lost twenty
pounds
that way."

"Where
do you think
they got a *Giganotosaurus*?"
asked Ryan.

"They probably
went to Rent-a-
Dinosaur,"
Michael said. "You
can rent anything."

Next to the
Giganotosaurus was a big bear
that was standing up on its
hind legs like it was about to

attack. It was cool, and scary.

Ryan's mom and the other grown-ups told us to spread out our sleeping bags on the floor underneath *Giganotosaurus*. Then they went off to do boring grown-up stuff, like drink coffee and talk about the weather. What's up with that? Grown-ups are always drinking coffee and talk-ing about the weather. I tasted coffee once, and I thought I was gonna throw up. But if they didn't drink coffee and talk about the weather, I don't know *what* grown-ups would do all day. They're weird.

Speaking of grown-ups, I wrote a poem about my dad. It goes like this:

*My dad has hair growing out of his
  nose.
If he didn't cut it, it would reach his
  toes.
He also has hair coming out of his
  ears.
I tried to tell him, but he couldn't
  hear.
Why do men grow hair in such
  strange places?
I thought it was weird when it grew
  on their faces.*

I unrolled my sleeping bag right next to
Ryan's. Then I turned around and saw . . .
THE COOLEST THING IN THE

HISTORY OF THE WORLD!

I'm not gonna tell you what it was.

Okay, okay, I'll tell you. But you have to read the next chapter. So nah-nah-nah boo-boo on you!

Wild Yak Attack

4

It was a candy machine!

"We want candy!" everybody started chanting. "We want candy!"

All the grown-ups came running over from wherever they were drinking coffee and talking about the weather.

"We're not here to eat candy," Mr. Docker told us. "We're here to learn about dinosaurs and natural history."

"I could learn a lot more about dinosaurs and natural history if I had candy," I told him.

"No!"

Sheesh, what an old grouch! Mr. Docker probably knows a lot about dinosaurs because they were around when he was a kid.

We were all grumbling about the candy when I suddenly noticed something out of the corner of my eye. It was even *more* amazing than a candy machine. It was a big, brown, hairy animal with horns and a hump on its back! It was standing very still right next to us.

"What's that?!" Neil the nude kid asked.

"I don't know," said Mrs. Daisy, who doesn't know anything.

"It's a wild yak!" said Andrea, who

knows everything. "I learned about it in my encyclopedia. Yaks live in Tibet."

"That yak wasn't here a minute ago," said Michael.

"Maybe it just walked over," said Emily.

"It can't *walk* over, dumbhead," I said. "It's dead."

Emily looked like she was going to cry. That girl will cry over any old thing.

"Hey, I think that wild yak just moved," said Neil the nude kid.

"It didn't move," I told him. "It's stuffed, just like the bear."

But just then the yak let out a weird yak sound.

"AHHHHHHHHHHHHHHHHHHHHH!!!" yelled all the boys.

"EEEEEEEEEEEKKKKKKKK!!!" yelled all the girls.

I thought I was gonna die. Everybody was freaking out. That's when the wild yak threw off its wild yak fur. And do you know what was underneath?

A lady!

She had glasses, dark hair, and a pointy nose. On her belt were a walkie-talkie and a flashlight.

"You must be the students from Ella Mentry School!" said the lady. "My name is Ms. Krup. I'll be your tour guide this evening."

"I almost peed my pants!" said Ryan.

"Sorry I scared you," Ms. Krup said. "I'm just so excited that you came to spend the evening with me in the museum. We're going to have so much fun!"

"Why are you wearing a wild yak fur?" asked Andrea.

"Well, the wild yak wasn't using it any-more," said Ms. Krup. "So I thought I would."

That Ms. Krup lady is weird.

Suddenly, the lights dimmed. "The

museum
is now
closed,"
somebody
announced.

It was a
little scary in
the dark.

Ms. Krup turned
on her flashlight. We all gathered around her.

"The museum is a magical place at night," she whispered as she gave each of us a name tag. "I'm going to take you on a journey. We're going to encounter some amazing creatures and see some incredible things. If you listen carefully, you can almost hear the sounds of the jungle, the forest, the desert, the mountains, and the ocean."

"I don't hear anything," I said.

"She said *almost*, dumbhead," Andrea told me.

"Well, either you hear something or you don't," I said. "You can't *almost* hear something."

"I wish I didn't hear *you*, Arlo."

I was going to say something mean to Andrea, but I didn't get the chance because a loud *BLEEP* came out of Ms. Krup's walkie-talkie. We all jumped.

"Ms. Krup!" a voice said. "*Tyrannosaurus*

rex is missing!"

"I'm on it, Chief!" said Ms. Krup. "Kids, we've got to find Rexy! Are you ready to go on an adventure?"

"Yes!" said all the girls.

"Can we kill it?" asked all the boys.

"It's already dead, Arlo!" said Andrea, rolling her eyes. "*Tyrannosaurus rex* has been extinct for sixty million years."

"Your face stinks."

I bet Ms. Krup was yanking our chain about that missing *T. rex*. Dead stuff can't run away. She was just trying to make the boring museum seem interesting.

"Follow me!" she said.

The Scary, Dead Zombie Buffalo

Ms. Krup took a bunch of flashlights out of a box and gave one to each of us. Then we went off to search for the missing *T. rex*. Everybody was whispering and slinking around like secret agents. It was cool. Me and the guys pointed our flashlights up from our chins and made scary faces at the girls.

"The first floor of the museum is where we keep most of our dioramas," said Ms. Krup.

"I had diorama once," I told her. "My mom gave me some yucky pink medicine and it went away."

"That's 'diarrhea,' dumbhead!" Andrea said. "You had diarrhea."

"So does your face," I said.

Those diorama things were cool. Each one was a little room with animal statues and scenery behind glass. We saw pandas, gorillas, monkeys, beavers, reindeer, bighorn sheep, polar bears, and a moose.

The sign next to the moose said it weighs a half a ton and eats 20,000 leaves a day. That thing should definitely go to Weight Watchers.

But next to the moose was a buffalo, and it was even *bigger*. We pressed our noses against the glass so we could see it better.

"It looks so real," Andrea said.

"It *is* real," Ms. Krup told us. "These animals aren't statues. They're the real thing."

"That means they're . . . *dead*?" asked Michael.

"That's right," said Ms. Krup.

Just then I thought I heard scary music playing in the background. It was like a movie I saw once. Somebody said the word "dead" and scary music started playing.

"I'm scared," said Emily.

"If that thing was a zombie buffalo," I whispered, "it could jump out at us. And then we'd become zombies, too."

"My uncle lives in Buffalo," said Neil the nude kid.

"Your uncle lives in a buffalo?" I asked. "Why doesn't he live in a house like a normal person?"

"It's Buffalo, New York!" said Andrea.

"I knew that," I lied. It would be weird to live in a buffalo.

"I know a song about buffaloes," Emily said.

"Would you like to sing it for us?" asked Ms. Krup.

Emily nodded and began to sing:

"Oh give me a home
Where the buffalo roam,
Where the deer
And the cantaloupe play. . . "

Well, everybody just about died laughing. I slapped my head.

"It's not 'cantaloupe,' dumbhead!" I told Emily. "It's '*ante*lope.' Cantaloupes can't play. They're melons!"

Emily started crying, of course. What a crybaby! I bet she would've run away, too, if there weren't scary dead animals all over the place.

Ms. Krup made us tell Emily we were sorry.

Next to the buffalo was another diorama with some skunks and an opossum in it.

"These are nocturnal animals," Ms. Krup told us. "Does anybody know what 'nocturnal' means?"

Needless to say, Miss Smarty-Pants-Know-It-All was waving her hand in the air.

"Nocturnal animals sleep during the day and come out at night," Andrea said, all proud of herself.

Why doesn't a nocturnal animal fall on

her head? I hate her.

"That's right, Andrea!" said Ms. Krup. "Some people claim that our nocturnal friends walk around the museum in the middle of the night."

"That's scary!" Emily said.

It is not. That girl thinks everything is scary.

Ms. Krup showed us the rest of the dioramas on the first floor. But we never found the missing *T. rex*.

"What's in *that* room, Ms. Krup?" Andrea asked when we passed a door next to the stairs.

"Oh, that's a *secret* room," Ms. Krup replied.

"Ooooh, what's in The Secret Room?" we all asked.

"If I told you," said Ms. Krup, "then it wouldn't be secret."

"PLEASE? PLEASE? PLEASE? PLEASE?"

Any time a grown-up won't tell you something, just say "Please" until they can't stand it anymore. That's the first rule of being a kid.

"Hmmm," Ms. Krup finally said. "Are you boys and girls really good at keeping secrets?"

"Yes!" we all shouted.

"Well," said Ms. Krup, "so am I."

And she started climbing up the stairs to the second floor.

Bummer in the summer!

The Hall of Dinosaurs

There were about a million hundred stairs to climb. But when I got to the top, I saw the most amazing thing in the history of the world!

No, it wasn't another candy machine.

It was the missing *Tyrannosaurus rex*!

"Aha!" said Ms. Krup. "There he is! Rexy, you are a naughty boy!"

"WOW!" we all said, which is "MOM" upside-down.

Rexy was AMAZING. Ms. Krup told us that *Tyrannosaurus rex* means "tyrant lizard king." She also told us that Rexy is twenty feet tall, but his arms are shorter than ours. And he only has two fingers on each hand.

"Look at his teeth!" said Ryan.

"They could crunch through bone," Ms. Krup told us.

"That thing would bite your head off in a minute," I said.

"Hey," Ryan said, "if *T. rex* and *Giganotosaurus* got into a fight, who do you think would win?"

"*Giganotosaurus* would kick *T. rex*'s butt," said Michael.

"No way," said Neil. "*T. rex* would kick *Giganotosaurus*'s butt."

"Neither of you is right," Ms. Krup said. "These two meat eaters would never fight. They lived millions of years apart."

"I still say *T. rex* would kick his butt," said Neil the nude kid.

There was a model *T. rex* skull that

we could look at close-up. I put my head in its mouth, and Ryan took a picture with his camera. It was a real Kodak moment. Then all the other copycats put their heads in *T. rex*'s mouth for the fun of it. Well, except for Emily, who was too scared.

The room was called the Hall of Dinosaurs. We got to see a stegosaurus and a triceratops, and some other dinosaurs too. We learned all kinds of cool stuff. Did you know that some dinosaurs swallowed rocks to break up the food in their stomach? Yuck!

We saw real dinosaur eggs and foot-prints too. Ms. Krup showed us how to make fossil rubbings that we could take home. She let us hunt for dinosaur bones in a big sandbox, but I didn't find any. Then she gave us dinosaur-shaped graham crackers for a snack.

"Dinosaurs are the coolest animals in the history of the world," I told every-body. "And we got to see them dead and in person."

"Kids can learn a lot from dead ani-mals," Ms. Krup said. "But we also have live animals at the museum."

"Live animals?!" Emily said, looking all scared.

"Sure," said Ms. Krup. "Follow me!"*

---

*How are you enjoying the book so far? Good? Okay, keep reading.

It's Alive!

Ms. Krup led us to a room with a sign over the door that said IT'S ALIVE! We went inside and saw lots of animals in cages: snakes, tortoises, South American poison dart frogs, and a blue-tongued skink. They were awesome.

"These animal friends help us teach

people about conservation and the environment," Ms. Krup told us. "They also help us learn to respect wildlife."

Ms. Krup led us into another room that was really cool because there were butterflies all over the place.

"Look! A Giant Swallowtail!" Ms. Krup said. "And there's a California Dogface! We have thirty different species. In here the butterflies are free."

"Great!" I said. "I'll take ten of them."

"That means they're free to fly wherever they want, Arlo," said Andrea, rolling her eyes.

"I knew that," I lied. Bummer. I thought they were giving butterflies away.

Next, Ms. Krup took us to the Creepy Critters Room. She was all excited, running from cage to cage to tell us about the Giant Desert Hairy Scorpion, the Funnel-web Spider, the velvet ant, and the Mexican Red Knee Tarantula. They were gross, but cool. I kept an eye on Mr. Docker, to see if he was going to eat any

of the bugs.

"Eighty percent of the earth's living creatures are insects," Ms. Krup told us.

"So you're in good company, Arlo," Andrea said.

I was going to say something mean back to Andrea, but I didn't get the chance because Ms. Krup pulled this disgusting brown thing with wings out of a cage and held it up for us to see. It was about four inches long.

"This is General Muffin," she said. "He's a very rare hissing cockroach from Madagascar."

"WOW!" we all said, which is "MOM" upside-down.

Ms. Krup told us that most cockroaches have eighteen knees. And they can live for a week after their head is cut off.

"What do they eat?" asked Emily.

"They eat girls named Emily," I said, and everybody laughed. Well, except for Emily.

"Cockroaches will eat almost anything," Ms. Krup said. "General Muffin even likes to eat candy."

"Why is he called a *hissing* cockroach?" asked Andrea, who has to know everything.

"Because General Muffin can hiss by pushing air through a hole in his tummy," said Ms. Krup.

"Make him hiss!" we all chanted. "Make him hiss!"

"The general only hisses when he's disturbed," said Ms. Krup. "But he's so used to being handled that he hardly ever hisses. Would anyone like to *hold* General Muffin?"

"No way!" we all shouted.

"Pssssst! A.J.!" Michael whispered. "I dare you to hold the cockroach."

"Forget it," I said. "I'm not touching that thing!"

"A.J., if you don't hold the cockroach, it means you love Andrea."

"WHAT?" I said.

I didn't see what holding a cockroach had to do with Andrea, except that they were both gross. I sure didn't want to hold a disgusting cockroach. But I didn't want anybody to think I loved Andrea, either.

I was faced with the hardest decision of my life. If I didn't hold the cockroach, the guys would think I loved Andrea. But if I held the cockroach, then . . . well, I would have to hold a disgusting cockroach!

I couldn't decide what to do. I thought so hard that my brain hurt.

"I'll hold it," I finally said.

Everybody cheered. Ms. Krup told me to put my palm out flat. Then she placed

General Muffin on it.

Ew! Yuck! There was a giant hissing cockroach sitting on my hand! I thought I was gonna throw up.

And that's when the most amazing thing in the history of the world happened.

General Muffin jumped off my hand!

We Have a Problem

"EEEEEEEEEEEEEEKKKKKKKKKK!"

"He's getting away!"

"Run for your lives!" said Neil the nude kid.

After General Muffin jumped off my hand, he ran under a table, so we lost sight of him. Everybody was yelling and

screaming and freaking out. You should have been there.

"Now look what you've done, Arlo!" shouted Andrea.

"I didn't do anything!" I shouted back at her.

Ms. Krup pulled out her walkie-talkie.

"Chief! We have a problem!" she shouted. "General Muffin is missing!"

"General Muffin is hissing?" a voice replied. "So what?"

"Not *hissing*!" Ms. Krup said. *"Missing!"*

We all hid in the corner while Ms. Krup searched for General Muffin on her hands and knees. She couldn't find him anywhere.

"I don't like this place," Emily whimpered. "I want to go home."

For once I agreed with her. I didn't want a missing hissing cockroach crawling up my leg.

The grown-ups led us down the hall into an auditorium.

"You'll be safe in here," Ryan's mom told us. "They're going to show you a video. We'll find General Muffin."

We watched a movie called *Our Reptile Friends*. We learned lots of stuff about reptiles. Like, snakes can still hear even though they don't have ears! So be careful what you say around snakes!

The video was pretty cool, but I still

don't want to make friends with any reptiles.

I was getting tired. Some of the kids fell asleep in the middle of the video. When it was over, the grown-ups came back to get us.

"Did you catch General Muffin?" we all asked.

"He's in a safe place," Ms. Krup said.

Whew! That was a relief. There was no way I would be able to sleep, knowing a giant hissing cockroach from Madagascar was running around.

Ms. Krup and the other grown-ups walked us back down to the first floor. Our sleeping bags were spread out under

Giganotosaurus, right next to the giant bear. It was gonna be cool to sleep next to a bear and under a dinosaur. And the best part was that we didn't have to brush our teeth.

The grown-ups drank some coffee and talked about the weather for a few minutes. Then they climbed into their sleeping bags too.

"Good night, everyone!" said Ms. Krup. "I'll see you in the morning."

"Good night," we all said.

"I'm scared," said that crybaby Emily.

"Don't worry," Ryan's mom said. "*Giganotosaurus* will protect you."

I didn't see how something that died

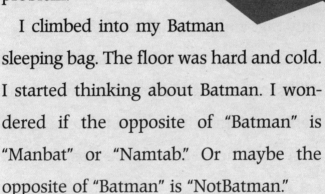

ninety-five
million
years ago
was going to
protect any-
body. But
that was Emily's
problem.

I climbed into my Batman sleeping bag. The floor was hard and cold. I started thinking about Batman. I wondered if the opposite of "Batman" is "Manbat" or "Namtab." Or maybe the opposite of "Batman" is "NotBatman."

I couldn't fall asleep. It was creepy looking up at *Giganotosaurus* in the dark.

So I thought about the cool dead and live animals we had seen. I thought about The Secret Room and wondered what was in it.

"Psssst! Ryan!" I whispered.

Ryan didn't answer. He was asleep. Everybody was quiet. You could hear a pin drop in the museum. I think I was the only one who was still awake.

That's when I heard it. A horrible noise! It was some kind of a monster! And it was right near me! It sounded like a giant nocturnal meat eater! And it was about to eat me alive!

Slinking Around

The horrible sound got louder and louder! It got deeper and deeper. I thought I was gonna die. Finally, I climbed out of my sleeping bag to see what was making all that noise.

It was Mr. Docker and Mr. Macky! They

were snoring!

I thought I was in the middle of a herd of hippos! Man, what is the problem with grown-ups? Kids don't snore like that. It must have something to do with the hair growing out of their noses.

I hope I never grow up to be a

grown-up.

"Pssssst! A.J.!" Michael whispered. "Are you up?"

"Yeah!"

"I can't sleep with all this snoring," Michael said.

"Me neither."

That's when I got the greatest idea in the history of the world.

"Hey," I said. "You wanna go get candy?"

"Do you have any money?" Michael asked.

"No. Do you?"

"No."

Bummer in the summer! I really

wanted candy.

"Let's go get a drink from the water fountain," Michael whispered.

"Okay!"

I stepped over a few kids in sleeping bags, and then my foot bumped into something hard.

"Owwww!" somebody yelled. "You kicked me in the head, Arlo!"

Ugh, it was Andrea!

"*SOR*-reeee!" I said.

Whenever you have to say you're sorry to someone but you don't really feel sorry, just say "*SOR*-reeee." Because "*SOR*-reeee" is the opposite of "sorry." When you say "*SOR*-reeee," it means you're not sorry at all. But nobody can punish you, because at least you did say you were sorry. So it's a win-win! That's the first rule of being a kid.

"Do you have any money?" Michael asked Andrea.

"Of course," she replied. "My mother gave me a ten-dollar bill to buy something educational at the gift shop."

Everything Andrea does is educational. When she blows her nose, she probably writes an essay about boogers for extra credit.

"Can we borrow some of your money?" I asked. "We wanna get candy."

"Only if I can get some, too," she replied.

I didn't want Andrea coming with us to the candy machine, but I did want candy.

"Okay," I said.

"I have money too," a voice whispered. "I want to come."

Oh, man! It was that crybaby Emily. This thing was turning into a party.

The four of us grabbed our flashlights and tiptoed around the other sleeping bags.

"Hey, you know what would be cool?" I said. "We should pick up one of the snoring grown-ups and put them in a diorama! Can you imagine Mr. Docker or Mr. Macky waking up next to a wild yak?"

"That would be hilarious," Michael

agreed. "But I don't think we could pick them up."

"We could if they went to Weight Watchers," I told him.

"Can we *go* already?" said Andrea.

The four of us slinked around in the dark like secret agents.

"How come they don't have a security guard?" Emily whispered. "Anybody could come in here and murder us."

"The doors are locked, dumbhead," I told her. "They have chains on them."

"If there are chains on the door," Michael whispered, "that means we can't get *out*, either."

We all looked at each other. I thought I

heard scary music playing again.

"Relax," I finally said. "Who's gonna murder us? The dead animals?"

We slinked over to the candy machine. Awesome! It had all my favorite candy bars. This was the best night of my life!

Andrea put her ten-dollar bill in the slot, but it popped back out. She tried it again, and it popped out again.

"The machine doesn't take ten-dollar bills," Andrea said.

This was the worst night of my life!

"Hey, look!" Michael said, pointing to some boxes that were stacked next to the candy machine.

"They're boxes of candy!" said Emily.

"Great!" Michael said. "The candy is free!"

"You mean it can fly wherever it wants?" I asked.

"No, dumbhead," Andrea told me. "It

means they're *giving* the candy away."

All right! I was so happy, I didn't even bother saying anything mean to Andrea. We all grabbed the candy and started stuffing it in our mouths. I ate about a million hundred candy bars.

It was the greatest night of my life.

Penguins Are Cool

It was dark and quiet. The little hand on the clock was past twelve, so I knew it was after midnight. But I ate so much sugar, there was no way I was going to get to sleep.

"Let's slink around by the animals!" I suggested.

"Yeah!" agreed Michael.

"You're going to get in trouble," Andrea said.

"I'm going to tell Mrs. Daisy," said Emily.

"Fine," I said. "Tell her. And I'll tell her that *you* ate all that candy."

Me and Michael slinked around the first floor like secret agents. Andrea and Emily, the big copycats, followed us. We looked at the moose again, and the buffalo and the gorillas. The animals looked even *more* real late at night.

That's when I saw it. The most amazing thing in the history of the world.

But I'm not going to tell you what it was.

Okay, okay, I'll tell you. And you don't even have to read the next chapter.

It was a diorama filled with penguins!

Penguins! I must have missed this before. I'm sure I would have remembered it.

I pressed my nose against the glass. Ever since I was little, I loved penguins. I slept with a stuffed penguin in my crib when I was a baby. I dressed up like a penguin for Halloween. I used to have an imaginary penguin friend. I saw every penguin movie there was to see.

Looking at those penguins close-up, I was hypnotized. I could almost hear them speaking to me.

"Come with us, A.J.!" one of the penguins said. "We'll go to Antarctica! You can play with us forever and ever and ever."

"Kids don't have to go to school in Antarctica," said the second penguin. "There are no teachers to tell you what to do. There are no parents to yell at you. There are no problems. It's paradise."

"In Antarctica we don't care if you

secretly love Andrea," said the third penguin.

"Come with us and live in peace," said the fourth penguin. "We'll slide around on the ice all day. It'll be fun."

"I'm coming," I told the penguins. "I'm coming with you. . . ."

Suddenly, I felt a hand on my shoulder. It was Michael's.

"A.J., are you okay?" he asked. "Who are you talking to, man?"

"Uh, nobody."

It must have been the sugar.

How to Stuff Stuff

We slinked around some more, and then I came up with the greatest idea in the history of the world.

"Hey!" I said. "Let's see what's in The Secret Room!"

"A.J., you're a genius!" Michael said.

Andrea and Emily said we would get in

trouble. But me and Michael slinked over to The Secret Room, and the copycat sisters followed us.

Michael put his hand on the doorknob.

"Don't open that door!" I warned.

"Why not?"

"Because when you open a door to a scary place at night, a horrible creature is waiting to jump out and kill you," I told him. "I saw that in a movie once."

"That's silly," Andrea said. She grabbed the knob and pulled open the door.

You'll never believe in a million hundred years what was in The Secret Room.

It was Ms. Krup! She was holding that wild yak fur.

"What are you kids doing here?" she asked.

I didn't know what to say. I didn't know what to do. I had to think fast.

"We're . . . uh . . . sleepwalking," I said.

"*All* of you?"

"It's dangerous to sleepwalk alone," I explained.

"Are we in trouble?" asked Andrea, who I'm sure has never been in trouble in her whole life.

"Of course not," Ms. Krup said. "You kids must love natural history, just like I do. When I was your age, I snuck into a zoo one night."

People who sneak into zoos at night

are weird.

"You must be nocturnal," Michael said.

We looked around The Secret Room. There were heads and other parts of dead animals everywhere. It was creepy.

"What *is* this place?" Emily asked.

"This is where we prepare the animals," Ms. Krup told us. "You see, I'm a part-time taxidermist. Do you know what a taxider-mist does?"

"You drive people to the airport?" I guessed.

"That's a taxi driver, dumbhead!" Andrea said. "Taxidermists mount ani-mals for display."

"Oh, yeah?" I told Andrea. "Well, maybe she mounts animals for display and *then* she drives them to the airport."

Ha-ha-ha! In her face! That's why I'm in the gifted and talented program. Nah-nah-nah boo-boo on Andrea.

"So, you stuff stuff?" Michael asked Ms. Krup.

"The animals aren't stuffed," she told us. "The skin is mounted on its original skeleton, which is covered with wire and plaster. I try to make dead animals come to life."

People who make dead animals come to life are weird.

"Taxidermy is cool," said Andrea, the big brownnoser.

"Hey," Ms. Krup said, "would you kids like to see a *special* exhibit I'm working on? It isn't even open to the public yet."

"Sure!" we all said.

"Follow me!"

Ms. Krup led us down the hall to an unmarked door. She put a key in the lock. Then she turned the doorknob.

"Don't open that door!" I shouted.

"Will you calm down, A.J.?" said Emily.

Ms. Krup opened the door. There was a big sign on the wall. This is what it said:

THE AMAZING WORLD OF POOP!

The Amazing World of Poop

12

I looked around the room. It was a whole exhibit devoted to poop! Nothing but poop!*

"I never thought I'd see poop in a museum," Emily said.

---

*Do you know what you get if you put poop in a toaster? Poop tarts!

"Oh, poop is a fascinating part of natural history," Ms. Krup told us.

We all laughed, because whenever a grown-up says "poop," you can't help but laugh.

Ms. Krup cracks me up!

"Poop can reveal what an animal eats, how it digests food, and whether or not it's sick," Ms. Krup said. "Some animals use poop to tell enemies to stay away. Others use it like perfume to attract mates."*

"Ew!" we all said. "Gross!"

Ms. Krup walked around and showed us the displays she made. I had never

---

*That stuff must be called Chanel No. 2.

seen anyone who was so excited about poop.

"Did you know that the most expensive coffee in the world comes from Palm Civet poop in Indonesia?" Ms. Krup asked us. "It costs a hundred and seventy-five dollars a pound."

"I'm glad my parents drink tea," said Michael.

"Really?" Ms. Krup said. "In China they make some tea from caterpillar poop."

"That's the last time I go to a Chinese restaurant!" I exclaimed.

Ms. Krup showed us a picture of a sloth. "It only poops once a week," she said.

"That happened to my dad once," said

Emily. "He had to go to the doctor."

"A week isn't so long," Ms. Krup told us.

"Grizzly bears may go six *months* without pooping."

"No wonder they're so mad!" I said.

"African elephants can produce three hundred pounds of poop every day!" Ms. Krup said.

"Wow!" said Andrea. "What do they do with all that poop?"

"Well, in some parts of Africa and Asia, elephant poop is made into paper."

"I hope they don't make it into toilet paper," I said. "Because that would just be weird."

"Do you know what else is weird?" Ms. Krup said. "Rabbits eat their *own* poop!"

"Ew, disgusting!" we all shouted.

"And termites glue their houses together with poop."

"Hey, Andrea," I said, "didn't your dad do that to your house?"

"Oh, snap!" said Michael.

"That's mean, Arlo!"

"Dung beetles push balls of poop around and bury it," Ms. Krup told us.

"Sounds like one of Arlo's playdates," Andrea said.

"Oh, snap!" said Michael.

"Storks squirt poop on their legs in hot weather to cool off," Ms. Krup said.

"So does Andrea," I said.

We pushed buttons to watch cool videos of animals pooping. Did you know that a rhinoceros stomps on its poop and kicks it around? It's hilarious. And some boy cranes fling buffalo poop up in the air to impress girl cranes.

"Don't even *think* about it, Arlo," said Andrea.

"People throw poop around, too," Ms. Krup told us. "In Wisconsin they have cow chip–tossing contests. One man

Hey!

Ooooh! He's dreamy!

threw a cow chip more than half the length of a football field."

"Remind me not to play football on *that* field," said Michael.

"People in Wisconsin are weird," I said.

I had no idea that poop could be so interesting. We got to match poop samples with the animals that pooped them. Then we got to touch an eighty-million-year-old piece of dinosaur poop. Ms. Krup showed us some poop under a microscope too. And we got to push buttons on a map to learn the word for "poop" in different countries.

"Poop is a palindrome," Ms. Krup said. "Does anybody know what a palindrome is?"

Andrea was waving her dumb hand in the air like she had to go to the bathroom really badly, which would have made perfect sense in "The Amazing World of Poop"! But Ms. Krup called on me instead. So nah-nah-nah boo-boo on Andrea.

"A palindrome is when you make friends with bees," I said. "My pal is a drone."

"Not exactly," Ms. Krup said. "Andrea?"

"A palindrome is a word that's spelled the same way forward and backward," she said.

"That's right!"

Why can't three hundred pounds of elephant poop fall on Andrea's head forward and backward?

"You sure know a lot about poop, Ms. Krup," said Emily.

"Poop is my life," Ms. Krup replied.

People who like poop that much are weird. But "The Amazing World of Poop" was really cool. We learned more than anybody would ever want to know about poop. And Ms. Krup said the word "poop" so many times, it didn't even sound funny anymore.

It was really late. Ms. Krup took us back to the *Giganotosaurus*, and we climbed into our sleeping bags.

Finally, I fell asleep. I dreamed about a giant poop that was riding a bicycle. And it was making some weird sound. A buzzing sound. No, it was a swishing sound.

No, no, I got it. It was a *hissing* sound.

13

Stuff Like This Happens Every Day

What *was* that weird hissing sound?

"Hey!" I whispered to Ryan, who was in the sleeping bag next to mine. "Stop that hissing!"

"I'm not hissing," he replied.

"You are, too."

We went back and forth like that for a

while, until suddenly there was an ear-piercing shriek.

"EEEEEEEEEEEEEEKKKKKKKKK!"

"There's something in my sleeping bag!" screamed Emily.

Instantly, everybody was awake and jumping out of their sleeping bags. Emily started running around, freaking out.

"What is it?" Andrea asked.

"Maybe it's a blue-tongued skink!" I yelled.

"It's a bug!" Emily shrieked.

"It must be that rare hissing cockroach from Madagascar!" screamed Andrea.

"It's General Muffin!" Michael yelled.

"Run for your lives!" shouted Neil the

nude kid.

Ryan's mom and Mr. Macky and the rest of the grown-ups tried to calm everybody down, but it was no use. Nobody wanted the cockroach to touch them. We

were all screaming and jumping around. Finally, Ms. Krup came running over.

"What's the matter?" she yelled.

"That disgusting cockroach was in Emily's sleeping bag!" Andrea shouted. "Now we can't find it! I thought you said you captured it."

"I just said General Muffin was in a safe place," Ms. Krup explained. "I didn't want you kids to be scared."

"Well, we're scared *now*!" Andrea shouted.

"Poor General Muffin," said Ms. Krup.

"Who cares about General Muffin?" Andrea yelled. "It's a cockroach!"

Man, that was a first. Andrea actually

yelled at a grown-up!

"There it is!" Michael suddenly shouted. "There's the cockroach!"

"Where?"

"There!"

"Emily!" Andrea shouted. "It's crawling on your back!"

"EEEEEEEEEEEEEKKKKKKKKKK!"

"Let's kill it!" all the boys yelled, and we started chasing after Emily.

"Don't kill General Muffin!" shouted Ms. Krup. "He's very rare!"

"Kill it! Kill it! Kill it!" we all chanted.

Emily was running around like her pants were on fire, and me and all the other boys were chasing her. That's when

the most amazing thing in the history of the world happened. Do you remember that giant bear that was next to the *Giganotosaurus*? Well, while we were chasing Emily around, Neil the nude kid—he . . . uh . . . ran into it.

"Watch out!" Ryan's mom yelled.

The giant bear started to topple over. And do you know where it landed? Right on Emily!

It was hilarious. A real Kodak moment. You should have been there.

"EEEEEEEEEEKKKKKKKKKK!" Emily

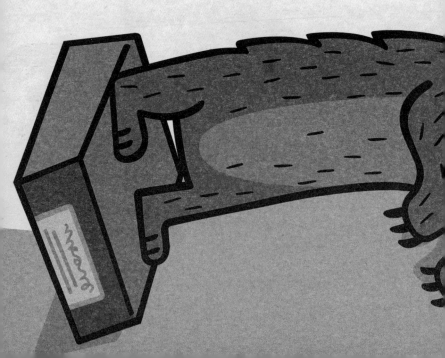

screamed, freaking out on the floor. "There's a dead bear on me! Get it off! Get it OFF!"

Sheesh, what a crybaby! So there was a giant hissing cockroach in her sleeping bag and a dead bear fell on top of her. Big deal. Stuff like that happens all the time.

Finally, Mr. Macky and Mr. Docker were able to pull the bear off Emily. Ms.

Krup caught General Muffin with a net and put him in a cage.

After all the excitement was over, the grown-ups brought us into a room for breakfast. They gave us cow chips and scrambled dinosaur eggs, but I don't think they were real.

"I hate natural history," Emily said.

"Natural history is cool," said Michael.

We were still eating when Ms. Krup came running into the room.

"Hey, who ate all the candy that was next to the candy machine?" she asked.

I looked at Michael. Michael looked at Andrea. Andrea looked at Emily. Emily looked at me.

"It must have been General Muffin," I lied.

"Yeah," Michael said. "You told us he likes candy."

We probably shouldn't have lied about General Muffin eating the candy. But Ms. Krup shouldn't have lied to us about capturing General Muffin. Lying isn't a very nice thing to do. But I guess sometimes even grown-ups do it.

"The museum will open in five minutes," somebody announced.

It was time for us to leave. We rolled up our sleeping bags. Ryan's mom said we could look in the gift shop for a few minutes until Mrs. Kormel arrived with the bus. Andrea felt bad about what happened to Emily, so she bought her a glow-in-the-dark dinosaur bone toothbrush. Neil the nude kid bought a box of fake moose poop that was really just chocolate.

As we were leaving the museum, Ms. Krup gave each of us a diploma that said we were Junior Nature Lovers. There was a picture of a dinosaur on it. I'm going to put mine up in my bedroom.

All in all, the natural history museum was almost not boring.

"Can we come back next week?" I asked Ms. Krup as we lined up at the door.

"Uh, well," said Ms. Krup, "now that you are official Junior Nature Lovers, you . . .

uh . . .

don't have to

EVER come back here

again."

"Bingle boo," said Mrs. Kormel as we piled on the bus to go home. "What did you learn about?"

"Poop," I told her.

Well, that's pretty much what happened on the field trip. Maybe Ms. Krup will never find out that we ate all the candy. Maybe General Muffin will stay in his cage from now on. Maybe someday Emily will forget that a giant hissing cockroach crawled into her sleeping bag and that a dead bear fell on her. Maybe Mr. Docker and Mr. Macky will cut their nose hair so they'll stop snoring. Maybe Ms. Krup will stop dressing up like a wild yak and get interested in something besides poop. And maybe we'll be able to talk Mrs. Daisy into taking us on another field trip.

But it won't be easy!

Don't miss the brand-new My Weird School Daze series starring A.J. and all his wacky teachers!

#1: Mrs. Dole Is Out of Control!

This crazed PTA president is turning graduation into a bigger affair than a presidential inauguration. Caps and gowns, a surprise guest speaker, fireworks, a petting zoo—by the time the ceremony is over, it will be time to graduate from next year's class!

#2: Mr. Sunny Is Funny!

A.J.'s summer vacation is ruined when yucky Andrea's family rents the beach house next door. Her crush on the lifeguard, Mr. Sunny, is driving everyone crazy!

HarperTrophy®
An Imprint of HarperCollinsPublishers

www.harpercollinschildrens.com